GW01236526

# FIRST WOMAN IN SPACE

Ben Hubbard

WAYLAND
www.waylandbooks.co.uk

First published in Great Britain in 2020 by Wayland
Copyright © Hodder & Stoughton 2020

All rights reserved.

Credits
Editor: Julia Bird
Illustrator: Alex Oxton
Packaged by: Collaborate

HB 978 1 5263 1354 6
PB ISBN 978 1 5263 1355 3

Wayland
An imprint of Hachette Children's Group
Part of Hodder & Stoughton
Carmelite House
50 Victoria Embankment
London EC4Y 0DZ
www.hachette.co.uk

Printed in China

MIX
Paper from responsible sources
FSC® C104740

# CONTENTS

| | |
|---|---|
| **SPACE AWAITS** | 4 |
| **A CHILD OF WAR** | 6 |
| **PARACHUTE JUMPS** | 8 |
| **COMPETING CANDIDATES** | 10 |
| **STAR CITY** | 12 |
| **COSMONAUT TRAINING** | 14 |
| **COSMONAUT NUMBER 1** | 16 |
| **LIFT-OFF PREPARATIONS** | 18 |
| **INTO ORBIT** | 20 |
| **AROUND THE WORLD** | 22 |
| **HELMET HEADACHES** | 24 |
| **BUMPY LANDING** | 26 |
| **SOVIET HERO** | 28 |
| **TIMELINE** | 30 |
| **GLOSSARY** | 31 |
| **INDEX** | 32 |

# SPACE AWAITS

Cosmonaut Valentina Tereshkova seemed confident as she strode across the launchpad to her spacecraft, *Vostok 6*. But inside, she was quaking with fear – she was about to be blasted from the Earth's surface to become the first woman in space.

Cosmonaut Yuri Gagarin had noticed Tereshkova's nervousness on the way to the Baikonur Cosmodrome. As the first man into space, Gagarin could sympathise. "I understand you. It's hard to be first," he told Tereshkova.

After the Second World War (1939–1945), the Soviet Union and the United States had emerged as the world's two great superpowers. Both were desperate to get their hands on the technology used in the German *V-2* rocket, a terror weapon that could travel further than any other missile. Over time, both the Soviets and Americans developed their own rockets based on the *V-2*. These were soon powerful enough to reach space. A competition between the two superpowers emerged, known as the Space Race.

In 1957, the Soviet Union stunned the United States by launching the first satellite into space, *Sputnik 1*. Desperate to catch up, the Americans launched their own satellite in 1958. In 1961, the Soviets again took the lead by sending the first man into space, Yuri Gagarin. This historic achievement was marked with wild celebrations in the Soviet Union. A few months later, the Americans sent American astronaut Alan Shepard into orbit. Sending the first woman into space was the obvious next step. On 16 June 1963, cosmonaut Valentina Tereshkova was about to begin this dangerous mission.

# A CHILD OF WAR

Valentina Tereshkova was born in 1937 and grew up in Bolshoye Maslennikovo, a village by the Volga river. Tereshkova's father cycled to work across the fields to his job as a tractor driver, while her mother worked as a milkmaid.

The family had little money, but their cow provided them with milk and they grew their own vegetables. Tereshkova's mother taught her to ride horses and, in the evenings, her father played the accordion. It was a peaceful country life. However, the 1930s would bring great change to the Soviet Union.

In 1934, Soviet leader Joseph Stalin seized control of the country and vowed to rid it of its 'enemies'. This led to Stalin's Great Purge – a reign of terror that resulted in the imprisonment or death of millions of innocent Russians. Then, in 1939, Stalin signed an agreement with German leader Adolf Hitler that led to the invasion of Poland and the start of the Second World War. To strengthen his territory, Stalin invaded Finland. Tereshkova's father was forced to join the Soviet army and was sent to fight in Finland.

Because Tereshkova's father was a tractor driver, he was ordered to drive tanks in the war. The winter of 1940 was particularly harsh and many Russian soldiers who did not die in battle instead perished from the cold. Tereshkova's father went missing in action and was never seen again. As well as being grief-stricken, Tereshkova's mother could not afford to feed Tereshkova and her brother and sister on her milkmaid's wages. The family moved to the nearby city of Yaroslavl, so that Tereshkova's mother could work in the textile factory there.

# PARACHUTE JUMPS

Life was hard for Tereshkova's family in Yaroslavl. There was little food and money was tight. As a child, Tereshkova sat by the railway line and dreamed of being a train driver and travelling from place to place. But instead, she left school when she was 17 and began working in the textile factory with her mother.

Tereshkova's workmate belonged to the local flying club's parachute group and tried to convince her to join. Tereshkova had always liked sports. In a magazine, she read about a female parachutist who fell through the air for a full minute before opening her parachute. "I was shocked," Tereshkova later wrote. "Could I learn to parachute? The thought flashed across my mind. And then I started to dream about my first jump."

In May 1959, Tereshkova, now a member of the flying club, made her first parachute jump. After a few moments of free fall, Tereshkova opened her parachute and drifted to the ground, as it billowed out above her. As soon as she landed, Tereshkova wanted to jump again. But she had been too hasty. "Why did you jump without a command?" a voice barked at her. In her excitement, Tereshkova had jumped too soon!

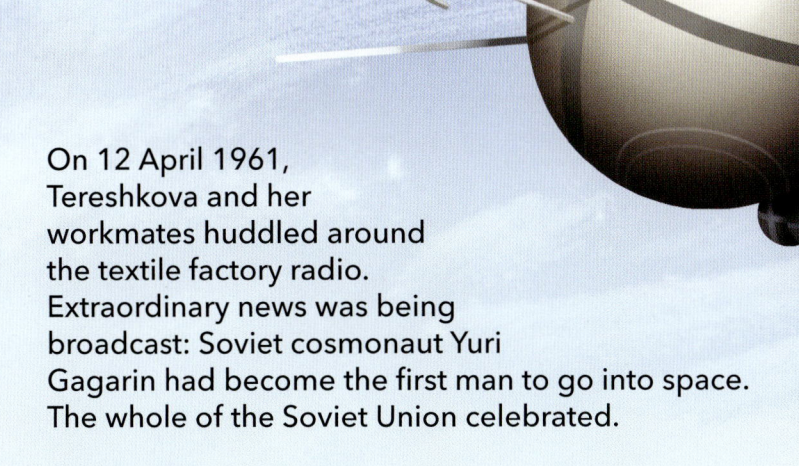

On 12 April 1961, Tereshkova and her workmates huddled around the textile factory radio. Extraordinary news was being broadcast: Soviet cosmonaut Yuri Gagarin had become the first man to go into space. The whole of the Soviet Union celebrated.

At home, Tereshkova's mother commented: "Now a man has flown in space, it is a woman's turn next." These words had a lasting impact. Tereshkova realised that she too wanted to be a cosmonaut. After all, Gagarin had come from a family of farm workers just like her. Tereshkova wrote to the Soviet Air Force asking that she be considered for cosmonaut training.

# COMPETING CANDIDATES

After Yuri Gagarin's space flight, every Soviet youngster wanted to become a cosmonaut. Over 400 women applied for the female cosmonaut programme, but only 23 were invited for a trial. Tereshkova was among them.

It was the idea of the Director of Cosmonaut Training, Nikolai Kamanin, to train female cosmonauts. He knew that to successfully send the first woman into space would be another Space Race victory. At a secret training centre, doctors X-rayed the women's bodies, studied their brain function and spun them around at high speeds. Only the best candidates would win one of the five available positions.

The candidates had to meet strict standards. They had to be younger than 30, shorter than 170 cm and under 70 kg in weight. They also needed at least six months' parachute training. The *Vostok* spacecraft was fully automatic, so they would not need to learn to fly it. However, during *Vostok's* descent, the cosmonaut needed to eject so that both she and the spacecraft could parachute separately to the ground. Parachuting experience was therefore essential.

The candidates included Valentina Ponomareva, an amateur pilot and maths whiz; and Irina Solovyova, an engineer and member of the national parachuting team. Both Tatyana Kuznetsova and Zhanna Yorkina were champion parachutists – Kuznetsova was a laboratory worker and Yorkina a teacher who could speak three languages. Tereshkova was uneducated and unskilled by comparison. However, she was a strong leader, an experienced parachutist and, importantly, a registered member of the ruling Communist Party. This would make all the difference.

# STAR CITY

In December 1961, Valentina Tereshkova received exciting news: she had been picked for the cosmonaut programme. However, the training was top secret. Few knew about the secret training centre known as Star City, hidden in the forest around 40 km from Moscow.

As well as physical training, Tereshkova had to study rocket theory and space engineering. Then she needed to prove her knowledge in the flight simulator, a replica of the *Vostok* spacecraft. Teaching the trainees was Sergei Korolev, the chief rocket designer. Korolev was a genius who had created the mighty *R-7* rocket that blasted the *Vostok* spacecraft into orbit. Without Korolev, the Soviet Union would not have been able to compete with the United States in the Space Race.

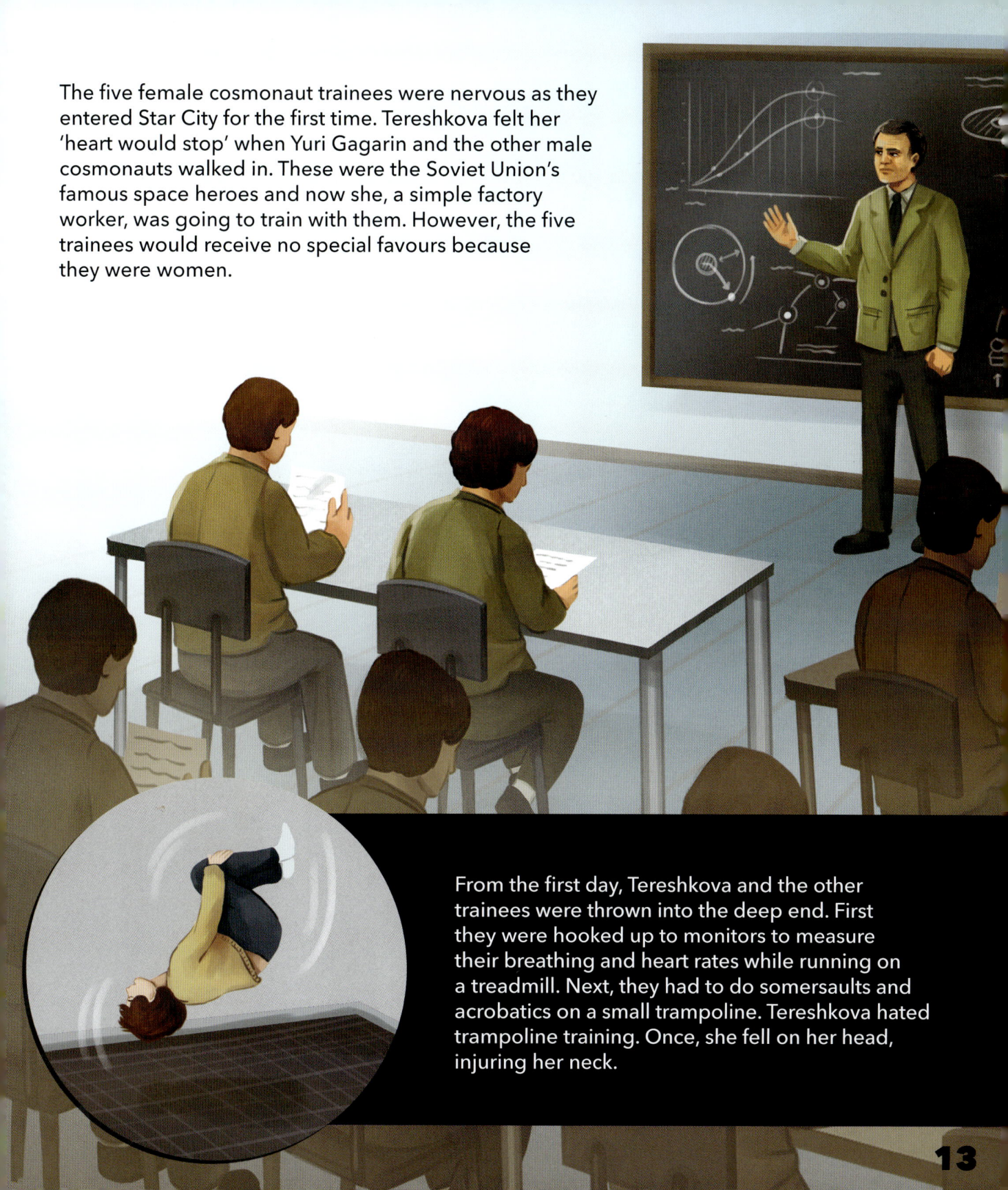

The five female cosmonaut trainees were nervous as they entered Star City for the first time. Tereshkova felt her 'heart would stop' when Yuri Gagarin and the other male cosmonauts walked in. These were the Soviet Union's famous space heroes and now she, a simple factory worker, was going to train with them. However, the five trainees would receive no special favours because they were women.

From the first day, Tereshkova and the other trainees were thrown into the deep end. First they were hooked up to monitors to measure their breathing and heart rates while running on a treadmill. Next, they had to do somersaults and acrobatics on a small trampoline. Tereshkova hated trampoline training. Once, she fell on her head, injuring her neck.

# COSMONAUT TRAINING

The training took nearly two years. During this time, Tereshkova and the other trainees were pushed to their limits. They learned how to fly MiG fighter jets, carried out over 120 parachute jumps and spent hours on the dreaded centrifuge machine.

The centrifuge was a large machine that spun a cosmonaut around at speed. The spinning got faster and faster, to imitate the high G-force felt during lift-off and landing. ('G' stands for gravitational.) Humans constantly experience 1 G from the Earth's gravity, but during space flights, cosmonauts could experience between 3 and 9 Gs. The scientists at Star City sometimes pushed the centrifuge machine to a terrifying 18 Gs.

After the centrifuge machine, the trainees were put in heat and isolation chambers. In the heat chamber, the trainees had to perform simple tasks in their spacesuits while the temperature rose to 70°C. In the sound-proofed isolation chamber, cosmonauts were locked away for ten days without contact with the outside world. During this trial, scientists studied the cosmonauts' emotional and physical behaviour. Tereshkova was allowed to take one book of poetry in with her.

Tereshkova made over 160 parachute jumps while training to be a cosmonaut. Her jumps included parachuting from a plane 5 km above the sea in a spacesuit weighing nearly 130 kg. She also learned to fly MiG fighter jets and took to the skies as a passenger in specially modified zero-gravity aeroplanes. These planes gave the trainees a few seconds of the weightless conditions they would encounter in space.

# COSMONAUT NUMBER 1

By late 1962, the gruelling cosmonaut training programme was taking its toll. Only Valentina Ponomareva, Irina Solovyova and Valentina Tereshkova were left by the end of the year.

The Russian government wanted one of the female cosmonauts to become a national and global celebrity. After his spaceflight, Yuri Gagarin had toured the world, winning people over everywhere with his smile and charm. At first, Ponomareva was the leading candidate to be first into space. However, Nikolai Kamanin, the head of the space programme, had doubts about her lifestyle.

On paper, Tereshkova was the weakest candidate but for Sergei Korolev, head of the female cosmonaut programme, this made her ideal. It meant the more skilled remaining candidates could be used on a later, more complicated two-person Voskhod mission. The final decision, however, was made by Soviet Premier Nikita Khrushchev. He liked Tereshkova because she had worked in a textile factory, belonged to the Communist Party and had a father who died fighting for the nation. Tereshkova was told she would be the first female cosmonaut to travel into space aboard *Vostok* 6 as part of a joint mission with *Vostok* 5.

Solovyova and Ponomareva were upset when they were told that Valentina Tereshkova had been chosen. However, Korolev assured them that they would travel into space soon. Solovyova was to be Tereshkova's back-up and Ponomareva would take part in a later mission. In fact, this did not happen. Korolev died in 1966 and no other female cosmonauts went on a space mission until 1982.

# LIFT-OFF PREPARATIONS

On 14 June 1963, Cosmonaut Valery Bykovsky blasted off aboard *Vostok 5*. Watching the launch from the Baikonur Cosmodrome was Valentina Tereshkova. She had just 24 hours to prepare to become the first woman in space.

Tereshkova was busy before her flight. Sergei Korolev met her and her back-up, Irina Solovyova, for a last briefing. Engineers gave Tereshkova a final tour of *Vostok 6* and all its flight instruments. Doctors checked her over one last time and kept her under observation.

On the morning of 16 June, Valentina got up at 7.00 a.m. and exercised. She ate a specially prepared breakfast and was fitted with sensors to measure her breathing and heart rate. Finally, Tereshkova walked to the bus and travelled to the launch pad.

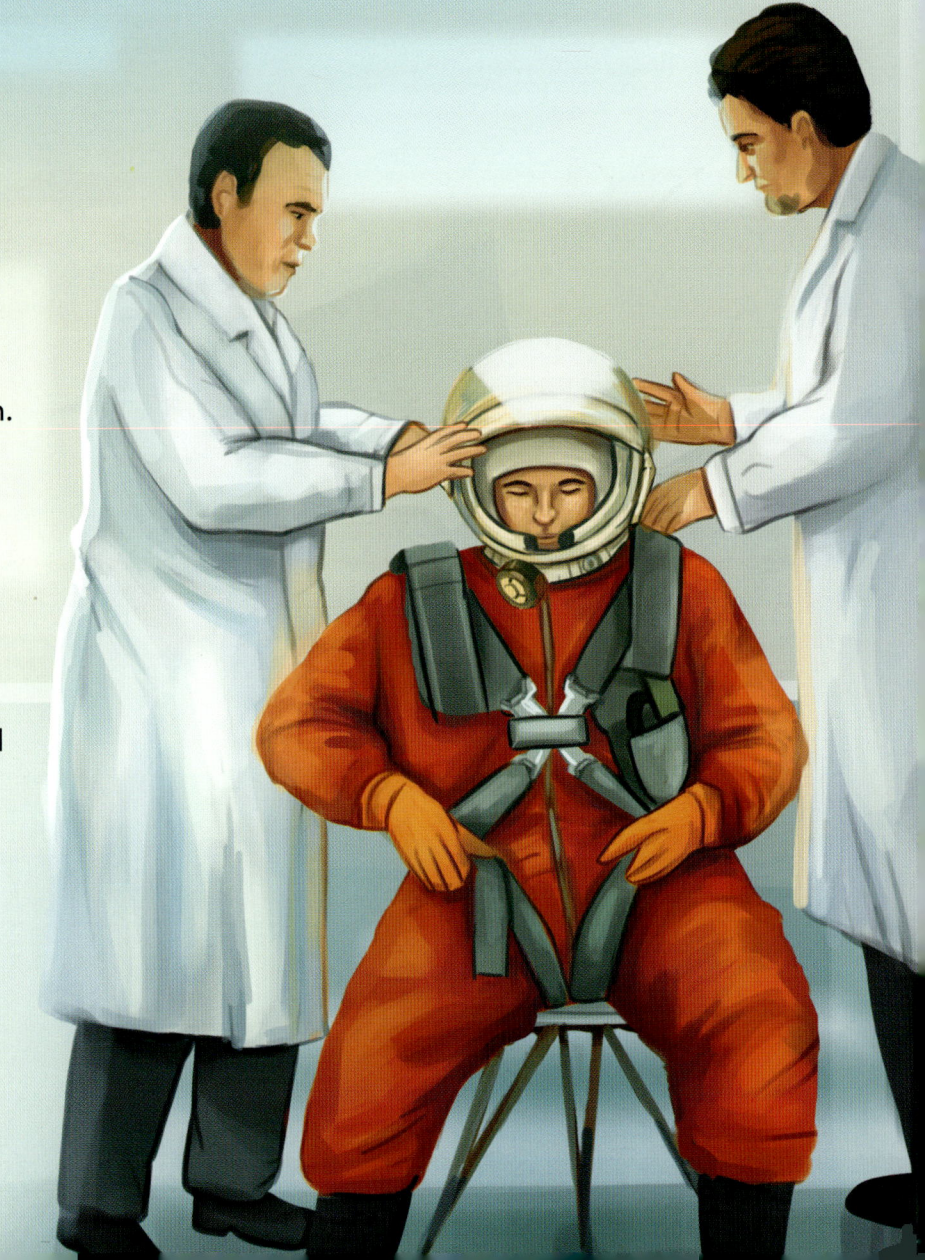

The *R-7* rocket worked by burning fuel and firing a jet of gas from its exhaust nozzles. This shot the rocket upwards to reach the speed of 40,000 kilometres per hour needed to break away from Earth's gravity and into orbit. Parts of the rocket, called stages, would fall away as the rocket blasted upwards, until only the *Vostok 6* spacecraft was left. Once in orbit, *Vostok 6* would circle Earth until its retro-rockets fired to slow it down and bring it back towards Earth's surface.

The Baikonur Cosmodrome was the top-secret launch site that all the Soviet missions were launched from. Constructed deep in a desert-like region of central Kazakhstan, the cosmodrome was named after a town 320 km away, so that other countries wouldn't know where it was. At 7.30 a.m. on 16 June 1963, Valentina Tereshkova was escorted to the top of the launch tower and helped into *Vostok 6*. The hatch was sealed behind her. Then, the countdown to lift-off began.

# INTO ORBIT

Tereshkova had a two-hour countdown to the launch of *Vostok 6*. It was a long wait. At one point, a familiar voice came over the radio. "Seagull, Seagull," said Yuri Gagarin. "Are you ok?" Seagull was Tereshkova's call sign and she told Gagarin she was eager to begin lift-off. Finally, the moment arrived.

## 3, 2, 1 ... LIFT-OFF!

"Hey sky, take off your hat, I'm on my way!" Tereshkova yelled as *Vostok 6* shuddered and shook as it rose from the launchpad. A weight pressed against her chest and Tereshkova struggled to breathe as *Vostok* raced towards the edge of the Earth's atmosphere. After 89 minutes, Tereshkova watched *Vostok 6* separate from the *R-7* rocket through the spacecraft's porthole. She was now in the Earth's orbit. "I am Seagull," Tereshkova said over the radio. "I see the horizon ... This is the Earth. How beautiful it is!"

*Vostok* 6 was made up of an instrument module and a descent module. The two were designed to separate before re-entering Earth's atmosphere. When the time came, at 4 km above Earth, Tereshkova would activate the exploding bolts on the descent module's hatch and eject. Then Tereshkova and the descent module would parachute separately to the ground. Inside *Vostok* 6 was one simple control panel. The spacecraft was fully automatic so the only time Tereshkova would need to touch the controls was if something went wrong.

Tereshkova's first task was to make contact with *Vostok* 5. "Hawk, Hawk, I'm Seagull. Do you hear me ok?" Immediately Valery Bykovsky, or 'Hawk', answered from *Vostok* 5. The plan was for Bykovsky to be in orbit for five days and Tereshkova one. However, she was feeling well enough to agree to extend the mission to 2 days and 23 hours. Now that Tereshkova had made contact with *Vostok* 5, she started another of her tasks in space: taking photos of Earth's atmosphere. But Tereshkova was about to discover a terrible mistake with *Vostok* 6's flight coordinates.

# AROUND THE WORLD

As *Vostok 6* made its first orbit around Earth, people began to hear the news about the first woman in space. Tereshkova's family were shocked. Her mother thought she was away training with the national parachute team! As the world reacted, Tereshkova was experiencing a shock of her own aboard *Vostok 6*.

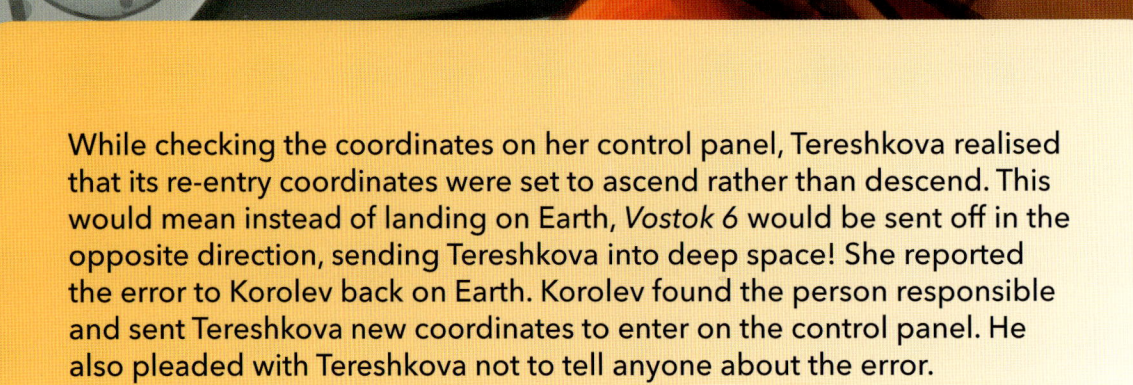

While checking the coordinates on her control panel, Tereshkova realised that its re-entry coordinates were set to ascend rather than descend. This would mean instead of landing on Earth, *Vostok 6* would be sent off in the opposite direction, sending Tereshkova into deep space! She reported the error to Korolev back on Earth. Korolev found the person responsible and sent Tereshkova new coordinates to enter on the control panel. He also pleaded with Tereshkova not to tell anyone about the error.

While in orbit, Tereshkova was asked to keep a flight log of her body's reactions to being weightless in space. "I tried to get used to the absence of gravity. I can't do it at once; it's too unusual for me," she later wrote. After a while, Tereshkova wrote that she felt sick, a common reaction to zero gravity. But her condition became worse when she tried eating space food from a tube. Tereshkova noted that the food was so disgusting that it made her vomit.

Meanwhile, Tereshkova was creating so many newspaper headlines that the Soviet leader, Nikita Khrushchev, wanted to speak to her. Over the radio, he congratulated Tereshkova on being the first woman in space and told her he would see her on Earth. The *Vostok 6* space mission had been a major success for the Soviet Union.

# HELMET HEADACHES

During Tereshkova's second day in space, the discomfort of being strapped into her seat for 71 long hours began to show. She began experiencing cramp and overwhelming tiredness.

After Tereshkova reported that she had been feeling sick, she was told to stay still. But this made her cramp even worse. Tereshkova was also developing an itchy rash under one of the sensors placed on her body. But her spacesuit prevented her from scratching the itch. The spacesuit helmet, too, was causing problems. The ring of the helmet was bruising her shoulder and the headset was making a loud, sharp sound in her ear.

Tereshkova would not be able to stay awake for 71 hours, but each time she drifted off, she woke up again with a jolt. A strange sensation had come over her. Then she remembered what Gagarin had told her about 'floating hands' in space. With no gravity to hold them down, Tereshkova's hands had floated up while she was asleep, giving her a start. She placed her hands under her seatbelt and fell into a deep sleep.

"Seagull, can you hear me?" crackled a voice over Tereshkova's radio. There was silence. The call came again, but still nothing. Korolev became concerned. He could see *Vostok 6* was still in orbit, but its commander had missed a scheduled status call. Finally, to everyone's relief, Tereshkova's voice could be heard. "This is Seagull, I am fine." Now awake, Tereshkova spent 15 minutes trying to exercise her limbs and wiped her face with a special space cloth. She had orbited the Earth forty-eight times. Soon she was ready for one of the most dangerous parts of the flight: landing. This is where all her parachute training would prove vital.

# BUMPY LANDING

From the beginning of *Vostok 6*'s descent, things were tense. Tereshkova had activated *Vostok's 6*'s retro-rockets to re-enter Earth's atmosphere, but had not been heard reporting this. Then, instead of being ejected at 4 km above the ground, Tereshkova was ejected at 7 km. It was going to be a bumpy ride.

After being ejected, Tereshkova was separated from her chair and her parachute flew open. Now she was being buffeted by high winds as she sailed towards the ground. Instead of land, Tereshkova was heading for a lake. Then, in the last few seconds, the wind blew her to one side and she landed heavily on dry land. As she hit the ground, her face crashed into the helmet, giving her a nasty bruise. However, Tereshkova had landed safely in the Altai region of Russia. Valery Bykovsky and *Vostok 5* landed three hours later. The Vostok mission was complete.

After landing, Tereshkova watched local farm workers rush towards her. They were astonished by the machine that had dropped from the sky and the strange being in a spacesuit that had fallen with it. Tereshkova walked to *Vostok 6* to grab a tracksuit to change into. The farm workers started to bring her food, including potatoes and bread. In return, Tereshkova gave out tubes of the space food she had so hated. Then she asked if one of them could drive her to a phone, so that she could phone Star City.

After being picked up, Tereshkova was flown to Star City for medical tests and questions about the mission. Her mission had been a great success, but mostly Tereshkova was pleased to be back on Earth. "When you are up there, you are homesick for Earth as your cradle. When you get back, you just want to get down and hug it," she said.

# SOVIET HERO

Sending the first woman into space was another victory for the Soviet Union in the Space Race with the United States. It would make Valentina Tereshkova a global celebrity for the rest of her life.

Hundreds of well-wishers greeted Tereshkova and Valery Bykovsky as they stepped off their plane at Moscow airport. Waiting for them on a podium were Gagarin, Nikita Khrushchev and members of Tereshkova's family. Tereshkova marched up to Khrushchev and said, "The commander of *Vostok 6*, Valentina Tereshkova has returned to Earth and can report the successful completion of her space flight."

The celebrations for Tereshkova's achievements continued in Moscow's Red Square, which was a sea of flowers and people. She was kept busy touring the world to talk about her spaceflight. Tereshkova made over forty-two trips in the first seven years alone. Her face was stamped on plaques and printed on postage stamps and pictures. Since her flight, Tereshkova has been given numerous awards including a Hero of the Soviet Union Medal and a United Nations Gold Medal of Peace.

Later, Tereshkova married fellow cosmonaut Andrian Nikolayev and they had the first child born to parents who had both travelled into space. Their daughter, Elena, trained as a doctor. Tereshkova herself continued to work for the space programme and retired in 1997 as a Major General of the Air Force. She then went into politics as a member of the State Duma, Russia's parliament. However, even with every achievement since, she remains known today as Valentina Tereshkova, the first woman in space.

# TIMELINE

**1944:** Nazi Germany fires its first *V-2* rockets at targets in France, Belgium and England.

**1955:** The Soviet Union begins constructing its top secret Baikonur Cosmodrome.

**1957:** The Soviet Union launches the first satellite into space, Sputnik 1.

**1958:** The United States launches its first satellite into space, Explorer 1.

**1959:** Textile worker Valentina Tereshkova makes her first parachute jump at the Yaroslavl flying club.

**1961:** Soviet chiefs Nikolai Kamanin and Sergei Korolev agree to train five female cosmonauts for missions into space.

**12 April 1961:** Yuri Gagarin becomes the first man into space aboard *Vostok 1*.

**May 1961:** The United States sends its first astronaut, Alan Shepard, on a sub-orbital flight.

**5 May 1961:** US president John F Kennedy announces that the USA will land a man on the Moon by the end of the decade.

**1962:** Valentina Tereshkova is selected to be the commander of *Vostok 6* for a joint orbital mission with *Vostok 5*.

**16 June 1963:** Valentina Tereshkova becomes the first woman in space.

**18 March 1965:** Cosmonaut Alexei Leonov performs the first spacewalk outside his *Voskhod 2* spacecraft.

**1966:** The Soviet chief rocket designer and head of the women's cosmonaut programme, Sergei Korolev, dies. His top-secret name is revealed to the outside world for the first time.

**24 April 1967:** Cosmonaut Vladimir Komarov is killed during the re-entry of *Soyuz 1*, when his parachute fails.

**27 March 1968:** Cosmonaut Yuri Gagarin is killed during an accident in a MiG fighter jet.

**1969:** The Soviet Union cancels its female cosmonaut programme.

**20 July 1969:** Astronauts Neil Armstrong and Buzz Aldrin are the first humans to land on the Moon, giving the US a final victory in the Space Race.

**19 August 1982:** Cosmonaut Svetlana Savitskaya becomes the second woman in space aboard her *Soyuz T-7* spacecraft.

# GLOSSARY

**Ascent**
The act of rising upwards.

**Astronaut**
A person who is trained to travel into space.

**Atmosphere**
The protective layer of gases that surrounds the Earth.

**Communism**
A political system that says all property is owned by the government or the community.

**Coordinates**
The numbers assigned to points in space, used to map the position of something.

**Cosmonaut**
An astronaut belonging to the space programme of Russia, previously known as the Soviet Union.

**Descent**
The act of going downwards.

**Flying club**
An aviation club that usually includes a landing strip, aeroplanes and hangars.

**Gravity**
The force that pulls people to the ground on Earth, and smaller celestial bodies to larger ones in space.

**Milkmaid**
A woman who milks cows and/or works in a dairy.

**Module**
A self-contained unit of a spacecraft.

**Nazi**
Short for National Socialist German Workers' Party, the political party in control of Germany from 1933 to 1945.

**Orbit**
The curved path an object takes around a planet, Moon or star as a result of gravity.

**Retro-rocket**
A small rocket found on a spacecraft, often used to slow it down.

**Satellite**
A natural or artificial object that is in orbit around a planet or star.

**Soviet Union**
The former union of Russia and fourteen other states, officially known as the Union of Soviet Socialists Republics (USSR).

**Superpower**
A strong and influential nation, such as the United States.

**Textile**
A type of woven fabric usually produced in a factory.

**Voskhod**
The Soviet programme to achieve a human spacewalk.

**Zero gravity**
The absence of gravity, which creates a sense of weightlessness.

# INDEX

Baikonur Cosmodrome 4, 18–19
Bykovsky, Valery 18, 21, 26

cosmonauts, female training programme 10–16

Finland 7

Gagarin, Yuri 4–5, 9–10, 13, 16, 20, 24
G-forces 14

Hitler, Adolf 7

jets, MiG fighter 14–15

Kamanin, Nikolai 10, 16
Khrushchev, Nikita 23
Korolev, Sergei 12, 17–18, 22, 25, 27

machine, centrifuge 14–15

Ponomareva, Valentina 11, 16–17

rockets
    *R-7* 12, 19–20
    *V-2* (flying rockets) 5

satellites
    'Sputnik 1' 5
Second World War 5, 7
Shepard, Alan 5
Solovyova, Irina 11, 16–18
Space Race 5, 10, 12
spacecraft 11–12
    Voskhod mission 17
    *Vostok 5* 17–19, 21, 26
    *Vostok 6* 4, 17–27
Stalin, Joseph 7
Star City 12–15, 27

Tereshkova, Valentina
    celebrations of her achievement 29
    childhood 6–8
    cosmonaut training 12–16
    factory worker 8–9
    joins a flying club 9
    later life 29
    learns to parachute 9, 11, 14–16
    marriage 29
    membership of the Communist Party 11, 17
    selection for cosmonaut training 10–12
    space mission 4–5, 18–27

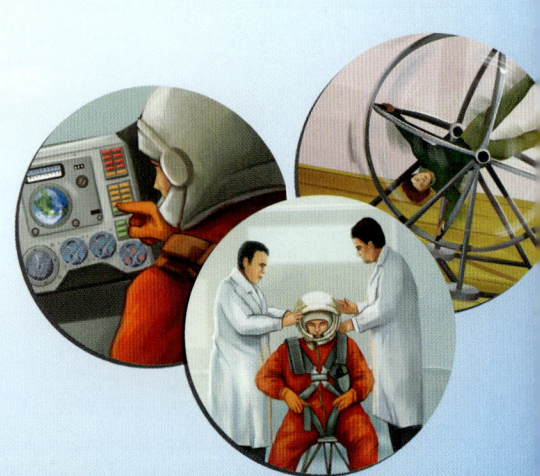

United States 5, 12